The Comical Celtic Cat

norah golden

COLIN SMYTHE
GERRARDS CROSS
1994

First published in 1984 by Brogeen Books,
an imprint of the Dolmen Press.
New edition first published in 1994 by
Colin Smythe Limited,
Gerrards Cross, Buckinghamshire.

ISBN 0-85105-505-2

Typeset in Victor Hammer's American Uncial
Printed in Singapore by Tien Wah Press (Pte.) Ltd

for my friends

&

special thanks
to
Chris * Phil * Jay

&

«speedwell»
the original comical cat

There once was a comical cat ...
There was ...
A comical Celtic cat.
He lived in Kells
The town of the bells
With a jolly old monk
Called Matt.

Now Matt was an artist by trade
He was ...
And a very good artist at that.
So he painted all day
And around him would play
The comical
Celtic
cat.

The cat was a comic,
    He knew he was,
And a proper old comic at that ...
    From his funny black nose
To his stubby white toes,
    If he knew Matt was watching
He'd sit up and pose
    With his face looking
                    fulsome
                    and
                    fat.

He sometimes caught mice
　　Which he thought very nice,
And carried them over to Matt,
　　Who'd leap from his chair
With a cumbersome air
　　And say something nasty
　　　　　　to
　　　　　cat ...

Poor cat would look sad
          For he must have been bad ...
(He looked sad in a comical way)
          So he'd gaze up and purr,
Meaning "Please stroke me, sir ...
          If you do I shall
                    bring you
                    a rat!"

Oh! what a comical cat you are,
What a comical
                    Celtic
                    cat!

Now, Matthew the monk
Was painting a Book
And the more he put in it
The longer it took ...

He'd done curly people

And fish with bright scales ...

And beautiful birds
with extravagant tails ...

A Saint called
St. Mark
with a sad
sort of
face

And letters
and spirals
all over
the place ...

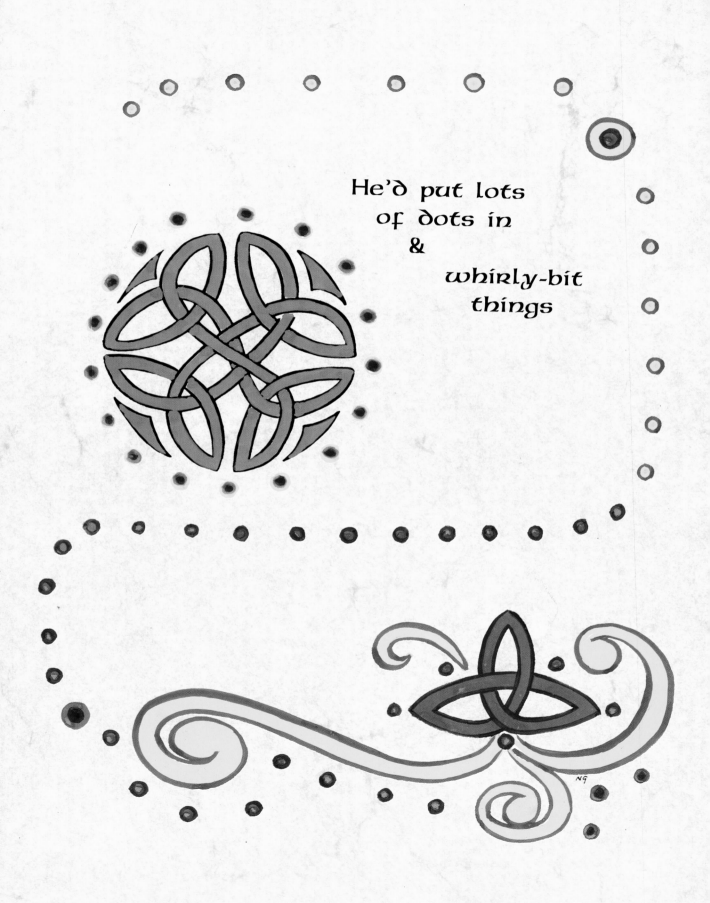

He'd put lots
of dots in
&
whirly-bit
things

And even
an elegant
Lion
with
wings ...

But he didn't know
    what to do next!

Poor Matthew he sighed
    For he'd tried and he'd tried
To find something new for the Book ...

Then he gave a loud shout
Knocked his paint-pots about
    And snatched up
        the comical
            cat!

"A capital letter you'll be,
    You'll see!
A capital letter ...
    A big letter C ...
Scratching your back
    Or biting your foot,
The most comical capital
        in the
            Book!"

Then cat had a week
    Of hard work, he had,
With never a moment to play.
    The monk made him pose
Biting four of his toes
    In order to paint him that way ...

No time to look fulsome and fat,
     Poor cat ...
No time to hunt mice
     For a snack ...
He was made to look thin,
     With his tail round his shin,
And his paws clawing
            up
              at
                his
                  back!

So the great Book of Kells
From the town of the bells
Was finished one day
By old Matt ...

And there in its pages
Till the end of all ages
Is the comical Celtic cat!

Oh! what a comical cat you are,
What a comical
Celtic
cat!